Papou's
PRETTY PIGS

Achilles Perry

Illustrated by Debbie Young

AuthorHouse™
1663 Liberty Drive
Bloomington, IN 47403
www.authorhouse.com
Phone: 833-262-8899

This book is printed on acid-free paper.

ISBN: 979-8-8230-4175-1 (sc)
ISBN: 979-8-8230-4263-5 (hc)
ISBN: 979-8-8230-4176-8 (e)

Library of Congress Control Number: 2025900489

Print information available on the last page.

Published by AuthorHouse 01/27/2025

authorHOUSE®

To the squirts and the maimous

Once upon a time there were three little pigs.

One was blue.

One was yellow.

One was blue and yellow.

The little blue pig
saw a young girl
selling jellybeans and
marshmallows.

He said, Ill
build my house
with these.

So he bought the jellybeans

red,

blue,

yellow,

and orange
jelly beans

and built his
house using the
marshmallows
as cement.
He saved four
marshmallows for
the chimney.

No sooner did the little *blue* pig finish building his house than along came **THE WOLF.**

Let me come in or Ill huff and puff and blooooow your house down.

Cool it, said the little *blue* pig. You arent getting in here, no how, no way.

THE WOLF started to huff and puff and puff and huff

soooo hard

that 17 jelly beans

flew off the wall

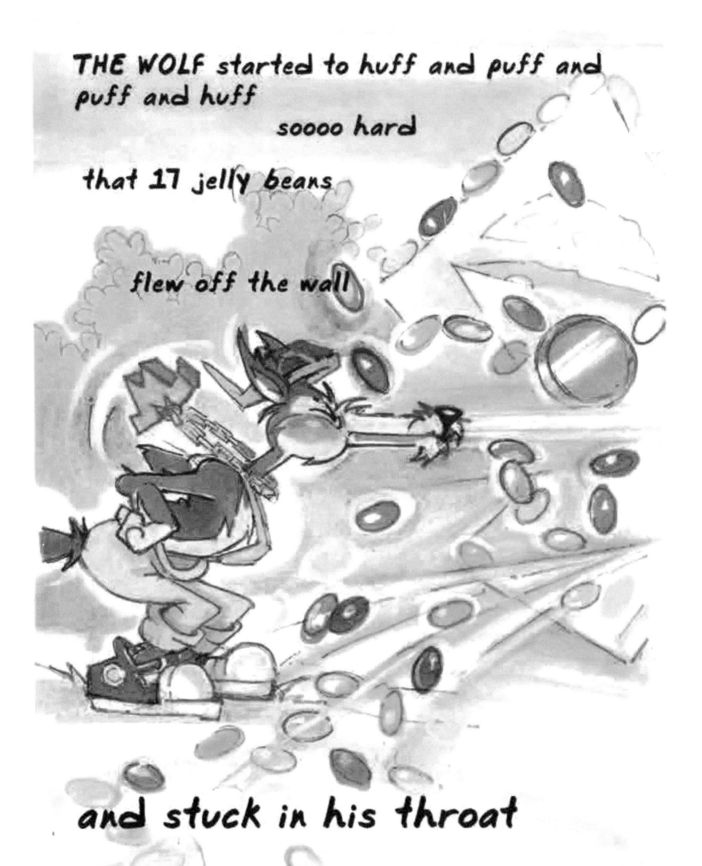

and stuck in his throat

Cough cough cough cough, went **THE WOLF.**

While **THE WOLF**
was choking the little
blue pig ran off.

In the meantime, the little yellow pig had found a boy with a candy cart. It was filled with lollipops of every color in the rainbow.

They were the biggest lollipops the little pig had ever seen.

He started by putting a row of lollipop sticks into the ground.

Then he licked the next lollipop and stuck it to the first row.

He licked and he sticked and licked and sticked until the house was finished.

Of course, he saved four marshmallows for the chimney.

No sooner did the little yellow pig finish building his house than along came **THE WOLF.**

Let me cough come in cough or Ill huff (cough) and puff and blooooooooow (cough, cough) your house down.

Cough,
cough,
cough,
cough

Cool it, said the little yellow pig. You arent getting in here, no how, no way.

THE WOLF started to huff and puff and puff and huff, but his throat was sore from coughing.

He had to get so close to the house that his tongue got stuck to one of the lollipops.

While **THE WOLF**s tongue was stuck to the lollipops, the little *yellow* pig ran away.

A little later on the little *blue* & *yellow* pig [which makes *green*] saw a truck filled with Chocolate Logs.

Oh, he said, Those will make
a wonderful house.
After he got the Chocolate
Logs he unwrapped the first
Chocolate Log and took a little
bite off of each end.

He did this again and again until
soon he had built a chocolate log
cabin house with, of course, a
4marshmallow chimney.

As usual **THE WOLF** shows up just as the log cabin is finished. His throat is still sore from the jellybeans.

His tongue has been stretched to four feet long from being stuck to the lollipop house.

But he comes again.

His voice is down to a scratchy whisper as he says, Little pig, little pig, let me come in or I'll huff and puff and blow your house in.

The little green pig says, Burp! He had eaten so many bites from so many Chocolate Logs, all he could say was, Burp, burp, burp, burp.

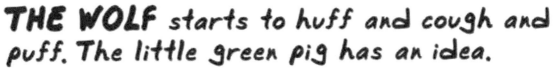

THE WOLF starts to huff and cough and puff. The little green pig has an idea.

He takes all the wrappers from the Chocolate Logs and makes them into a big ball.

Then he very carefully lights the ball.

It catches fire and the little green pig rolls it right at **THE WOLF.** He is so frightened he runs away **forever.**

The three little pigs lived happily until they finished eating their houses.

BURP!

Printed in the United States
by Baker & Taylor Publisher Services